A
BOOK
FOR
JODAN

D1360965

A BOOK FOR JODAN

Marcia Newfield

Illustrated by Diane de Groat

A MARGARET K. MC ELDERRY BOOK

Atheneum   1975   New York

Copyright © 1975 by Marcia Newfield
Illustrations copyright © 1975
by Diane de Groat
All rights reserved
Published simultaneously in Canada by
McClelland & Stewart, Ltd.
Manufactured in the United States of America
Printed by Murray Printing Co.
Forge Village, Massachusetts
Bound by H. Wolf, New York

First Edition

LIBRARY OF CONGRESS CATALOGING IN PUBLICATION DATA

Newfield, Marcia.   A book for Jodan.
"A Margaret K. McElderry book."
SUMMARY: When Jodan learns that her parents are
separating, she wonders what can be done to keep
them together and if she is to blame for their
decision.   [1. Divorce—Fiction]
I. De Groat, Diane, ill.   II. Title.
PZ7.N492Bo   [Fic]   74-18192
ISBN 0-689-50010-6

This book about people being important to
one another is dedicated to
Matthew, Sally, Susie, and *Judy Held*
and a man named Billy.

The author wishes to thank Stan Taylor
for his inspired creation of "Lullababy Lullabye" and
Elizabeth Arrigo for her patient transcription of it.
The photograph of the newborn infant is courtesy
of Garry Steinberg. The obstetrician is
Dr. Marcia Storch of New York City.

The illustrator wishes to thank her models,
the Haefeli family: Arthur, Jo Anne, and Lisa.

A
BOOK
FOR
JODAN

*J*odan loved telling people about her name.

"Well, you see it's an unusual name because my father made it up when I was born. He had just made sure my mother was all right and was taking a walk and thinking about being a new father and about me when this name came to him. It's a combination of the names of two people who were very important to him and my mother—his grandfather Joe and her father Dan. Jodan. It felt right to him because it had a lot of love in it. He turned around and went back into the hospital and told my mother the name he'd thought of. It felt right to her, too. The way to say the last part is *din*, *Jodin*, even though we spell it with an *a*."

Jodan was proud of having such a special name.

"No one else in the whole world is named Jodan, are they, Dad?"

"No one I know," he teased.

She wrote her name in big letters across the garage door.

Every night before she went to bed, Jodan and her father had a conversation.

Her father told her that when she was little she used to call them *conservations*.

Jodan would tell him about different things that happened to her—what her teacher had said, the story of a book she had read, and how she had decided to be a pilot when she grew up.

"Daddy, when you were nine years old, did you know that you were going to be a journalist?"

"No, I wanted to be a streetcar conductor."

Sometimes her father told stories of things that had happened to him when he was a little boy.

"Once I was playing in the woods with some friends, and we found a dead snake."

"What did you do?"

"We poked it with a stick to make sure it was dead."

"Was it?"

"Yes."

"Then what did you do?"

"We dug a hole and buried it."

"Were you scared?"

"You bet."

Jodan had good times with her mother, too.

They built bookcases together and collected tree leaves for a scrapbook.

"It's amazing, isn't it, Jodan? The trees have such different looks about them—even with their leaves half off. I like the huge old oaks the best I think. They seem so sturdy and reliable."

"The birch is my favorite," said Jodan.

"Yes, of course you would choose that," her mother said, looking at her fondly. "It looks like you—graceful yet strong." She tapped the brim of Jodan's baseball cap, "Come on, shortstop, we'd better go home now."

When they got home they put the leaves in a solution of glycerine so that they would keep their color and not get dry and crumbly.

On rainy days, Jodan and her friends rummaged through the attic. They adored the trunk of old clothes and costumes that Jodan's mother had kept from her college days.

They would dress up in long skirts and hats and shawls and come downstairs to show her mother.

"Cheerio, Mums, we're English ladies, about to sail on a Pilgrim ship. Can we have a spot of tea before we go?"

"My word, aren't you brave! You have a long voyage ahead of you. How about some hot chocolate?"

"That would be tops, just tops. Hope it's not too much trouble."

"Not at all, my chickadees, not at all. It's been good to meet you."

Jodan's mother's English accent was the most convincing. She said "not at all" so it sounded like "not tat tall." "Been" came out "bean." The girls practiced while they drank their hot chocolate.

On Sunday mornings, Jodan and her father would wake up early and make pancakes. Each time they put a different surprise ingredient in the pancakes. Then they would wake her mother and all eat breakfast in the living room.

Her mother would try to guess what they had put in the pancakes.

"Hmmm, it smells like a lemon, but it tastes sweet. Is it a lime?"

"No."

"A grapefruit?"

"You have to ask a question about it before you can make a good guess."

"Is it something that Grandpa Dan sent us from California?"

"Yes."

"Oranges!"

"You're right."

Jodan's mother usually guessed the secret ingredient because she was such a good cook herself. Whenever guests came to dinner, they kept talking about her cooking and saying she should open a restaurant. It made Jodan feel proud.

Jodan liked it best when they did things together as a family. They used to do things together all the time—sleigh rides, picnics, days at the beach. She remembered the summer after first grade when they had spent two whole months at the beach. Every night they made dinner outdoors over a stone fireplace and everybody helped.

Lately they hardly did any family things. Her mother and father always seemed to be arguing.

"When are you going to paint that ceiling? You've been promising to do it for weeks."

"I've been too busy. If you don't like waiting, why don't you do it yourself?"

"Because I'm tired of having to do everything in this house."

"Oh, leave me alone. Why don't you go call one of your friends and complain to them?"

Most of the time Jodan couldn't understand why they were shouting so loud about such small things, like who said what and whose turn it was to do the laundry. She wished she could stop it.

Once she tried. "Oh, stop yelling. I can't hear myself think."

"Jode, this has nothing to do with you. Close your door and do your homework."

Often she heard them arguing after she had gone to bed at night, and sometimes it was about her—how much television she should watch, whether she was old enough to go to camp. She would pull the pillow around her ears.

They went for an all-day hike in the woods. The first mile or so it was perfect. Everybody was happy and talked about the trees and the way the air smelled. But then her parents spoiled it.

"Did you put an extra pair of socks in my backpack?"

"No."

"But I asked you to."

"I forgot."

"I should have known you'd forget."

The rest of the way Jodan's parents hardly spoke to each other. It was hard to explain, but Jodan knew the difference between a happy silence and an unhappy one.

She didn't know which was worse—unhappy silences or loud, shouting arguments.

One afternoon in the zoo, they argued so loud that Jodan felt embarassed. Her father left, and she and her mother went to the reptile house by themselves.

Soon after that day, Jodan's parents told her that they were going to separate.

"What does *that* mean?" asked Jodan, feeling frightened.

"We're not going to live together anymore."

"What's going to happen to me?" asked Jodan.

"You and I are going to move to California," said her mother. "Daddy is going to stay here in Massachusetts."

"But *why*," said Jodan, "why can't we all stay together?"

"Mother's not happy living with me anymore, Jode," said her father. "She wants to try a different life."

"Now, that's not the whole story, Jodan," said her mother. "The thing is that we both love you very much, but our feelings for each other have changed. You know how much we fight. It's bad for all of us. It's just harder for Dad to admit it."

"You're probably right," said her father. "Yes." He nodded his head wearily. "You're right. It's the truth."

"But, Daddy, when will I see you?"

Tears came into her father's eyes. "You'll see me, Jodan. We'll write and visit." He hugged her to him. "We'll stay close. We'll find a way."

Jodan prayed that the separation wouldn't happen.

But it did, and she and her mother went off in a jet plane, leaving her father behind in the old house.

California was beautiful. It was warm and sunny, and outside the window was a shiny orange tree. There was a new school with a swimming pool and new friends to make.

Jodan got a lot of letters from her father and some phone calls.

She missed him, though. Every day.

What she wanted most of all was for her mother and father to get back together again. But her mother kept saying that it couldn't happen.

"But why not?" Jodan insisted after she had asked the question for the zillionth time.

"Your father and I don't love each other anymore."

"How can that be? I love both of you."

"That's different, Jode. We both love you, too."

"Then why can't you stay together? Why can't we live closer to Daddy?"

Her mother came and sat down beside her. "Jodan, I know it's hard for you this way. But it's what I needed. I needed to get away from him. Your father and I were making each other miserable. I couldn't live like that anymore."

"How can you say bad things about Dad?"

"They're not bad things. But it's true that your father's not a good husband for me anymore. That doesn't mean that he's not a good father to you."

Jodan hated her mother's calm voice.

"Why can't we live closer?" she raged. "Other divorced fathers live closer."

"Well, I thought about it a lot," said her mother, looking sad and troubled. "But I decided that I had to build a new life for myself and that I couldn't do it near him. I felt the best thing would be for me to come back here, where I lived and worked before I married your father and where I knew a lot of people and places. I felt it would be the best thing for you too, Jodan, to have a mommy who was happier. I wouldn't be much good for you otherwise."

Jodan put her head on the kitchen table, sobbing.

"NO, it's not better, it's not better!"

Her mother stroked her hair. "Jode darling, try to hear what I'm telling you. It has to be this way. That's what divorces are for—for people to start new lives the best way they can. And children have to go along with it. In the old days, parents who had stopped getting along stayed together for the sake of their children, and the children grew up without knowing that people could be happy with each other. Someday, when you're older, I think you'll understand that we've done the right thing."

"No, you haven't done the right thing!" Jodan shouted at her mother. "Haven't! Haven't!" She picked up the keys that were on the table and threw them on the floor. The chain broke and they went all over the kitchen.

"Jodan, stop it!" Her mother's voice had a warning sound. "I know you're upset, but you're acting like an infant. Now pick up those keys or I'm going to send you to your room."

Tears rolled down Jodan's face as she picked up the keys. "No! I'll never understand. I'll never understand about divorces."

And as she cried herself to sleep that night, she was sure that she never would.

Jodan's new friend, Hazel, picked her up every day on the way to school.

"What's the matter with you this morning, Jodan? Your eyes are all red."

"I was crying last night."

"Oh, did you have a bad fight?" Hazel asked sympathetically. She was the youngest of three sisters, so she knew about fights.

"Sort of like that," said Jodan. "My mother says there's no hope of her and my father getting together again. It makes me so sad."

Hazel put her arm around her friend. "Oh, Jodan, there are lots of kids at school whose fathers don't live at home anymore. My sister Clara's best friend's parents have a divorce. I'm sure your father loves you."

Jodan nodded. "I guess so. But he's so far away."

"Hey, aren't you supposed to visit him at Easter vacation?" asked Hazel.

"Yeah, I think so."

Jodan felt all choked up and was afraid she was going to start crying again.

"What does your father look like?" asked Hazel.

"Hazel, I don't want to talk about it anymore."

"Okay," said Hazel.

They walked for a while in silence. "What did you bring for lunch?" asked Hazel.

"Peanut butter and jelly."

"Oh, good, I brought tuna fish with red peppers in it. Do you want to trade?"

"Sure," said Jodan.

They parted for their separate classrooms.

"See you at gym."

That night Jodan wrote her father a long letter.

DEAR DAD,

I remember a lot of things about you. Our conser-vations and the way you make me laugh. But Dad I also sometimes have a hard time remembering exactly what you look like. Do you think you could send me a picture of yourself?

I want to show it to my friend Hazel.

Mommy said that you're going to send airplane tickets for me to come and visit you. I hope they come soon. I think about you every day. I am very lonely for you and sometimes I can't help crying. Can't you come and live here?

LOVE AND KISSES,

JODAN

A few days later a big envelope covered with stamps came for Jodan. It contained a typewritten letter from her father and a photograph.

HI JODE,

Here is the photo you wanted. Someday, when I'm visiting you, I hope I'll meet all your new friends. Right now, I'm planning for you to visit me—the date is set for when your Easter vacation begins. I've arranged to take a vacation from work, too, so we'll have lots of time together. In my next letter I'll send you the tickets. Now that's one good thing in all that's happened, isn't it, Jode? Getting to fly in an airplane all by yourself.

I miss you, too, and sometimes I cry about it. There's nothing wrong with crying when you're sad. We all hurt a lot from what we're doing now, yet I somehow feel it will in the end be the best thing. It's not possible for me to come and live there right now—maybe someday. I know it is very, very hard for a nine-year-old person to have her father so far away. It's hard for me to *be* away. But what you have to understand is that I love you as much as I always have. We can't share the same things that we used to when we lived in the same house—everyday things like good-night kisses and answers to questions and bedtime stories. But that doesn't mean that I'm not still your father or that I love you one bit less. What it does mean is that we have to think of different things to share with each other. I'm working on a surprise for you right now that I wouldn't even have thought of if we weren't far apart. I'll have it ready by the time you get here. I think you'll like it. And we'll think of a thousand other things to do together, Jodan. I know we will.

LOVE AND HUGS,

DAD

A week later the tickets arrived. And another letter.

DEAR JODAN,

The attendants on the plane know your name and will take good care of you. It's a long flight, so bring some books and things to do. It just snowed here, so pack warm clothing and wear your winter coat.

I'll be waiting for you as you come out of the plane. I can hear that nice laugh of yours now. Oh, Time, hurry up!

HUGS,

DAD

Jodan and her mother looked through her closet together to decide what clothes she should take with her.

"Mom, I want to take my new baseball uniform."

"But Jodan, that uniform's for here. Besides, it's still winter in Massachusetts."

"I don't care. I want to show it to Daddy."

"Well, in that case, I guess it's okay," said her mother. "Oh, look, Jodan," she said, holding up a pair of dungarees, "these pants are ripped. Come into my room and we'll make a patch for them."

Sitting on the top of her mother's bed was a big box wrapped in brown paper.

"Mom, what's that on your bed?" asked Jode curiously.

"Why don't you take the wrapping off and see?"

"Mom! It's a suitcase! With my initials on it!"

"I thought you'd like it," said her mother, smiling.

The night before her trip, Jodan was so excited she couldn't sleep. She kept thinking about the old house. And her father. And the airplane. A thousand thoughts raced through her head.

Her mother drove her to the airport to put her on the plane.

Jodan threw her arms around her. "Oh, Mommy, I want you to come and be with us."

"Now, honey, you know I can't. You go and enjoy your visit. I'll be here when you get back." She kissed Jodan good-bye.

A flight attendant took Jodan to the plane and gave her a seat. Jodan fastened her seat belt and watched people getting on. Her stomach felt funny. It was better after the plane got up in the air.

She slept part of the way, and the rest of the time she read books and looked out at the floor of clouds.

A lot of people were waiting at the terminal when she arrived.

Jodan didn't see her father.

"Jode, Jode, here I am. Over here!"

"Daddy!"

She raced into his huge hug.

Together, their smiles would have measured seven inches.

At first it felt funny to be together alone in the big house, but it got to feel okay.

They went ice-skating and to the zoo. They did a lot of talking and reading and laughing at television.

It was fun to cook pancakes together. And go to other people's houses for dinner.

Every once in a while Jodan reminded her father about the surprise that he had written he was making for her.

"Don't worry, Jodan, I haven't forgotten. I'm saving it for later."

As a special treat, Jodan's father taught her how to use his expensive tape recorder.

But sometimes she felt lonely.

"Dad, let's go to the park."

"Jodan, I'm reading the paper. Don't bother me now."

"But I don't have anything to do."

"Well, I'd like to be quiet for a while now. I'm sure you can find something to do."

"Oh, all *right*"—she pouted—"if I have to."

But she really didn't mind so much because it had been that way a lot of times before also.

She talked to her father about the separation. "Why can't you and Mommy get back together again?"

"It's too late, Jodan. It's over for us."

"But why? Why can't you just stop fighting?"

"It's not just that, Jodan. We were together for ten years. That's a lot of history. We can't go back. It's time for us to go forward in separate ways."

"Why can't you move to California?" she asked.

"Maybe someday I will, but now I can't. It's not practical. My work and life are here."

"But what about me?" said Jodan. "I'm part of your life, and I don't want you to be far away."

"I know, Jode, I know. You *are* a very important part

of my life. But you and I will work it out. See, you're here now, aren't you? And as you get older, you'll spend summers and. . . ." His voice trailed off.

Jodan bit her lip to try to stop the tears from coming. But it didn't work.

"Dad, I have to ask you a question."

"What?"

Jodan took a deep breath.

"Was it my fault?"

"Was what your fault?" said her father.

"The separation," said Jodan, surprised that he didn't understand.

He lifted her up, tears and all. "Your fault? Your fault? Not in a million years. If it wasn't for you, we would have split up years ago. Sweetie, we both still love you, we just can't live with each other anymore. Try to make the best of it."

Jodan sighed. Somewhere deep inside her she was beginning to realize that it was no use—she wasn't going to be able to get her parents to change, and they weren't going to be able to help her that much either.

One moonlit night the sky was covered with a lightness that seemed to touch everything on earth. Jodan and her father were driving home from a cousin's farm when they noticed a little wooden footbridge that went over a rocky stream. Jodan's father stopped the car on the side of the road.

"Come on, Jodan, let's get out and walk across the bridge. It's good luck to find a bridge this old."

He took her hand and led the way. It was a tiny bridge —twenty-five steps and they were across it. On the way back, they leaned over the side to watch the stream. Crisscrossed branches of the bare trees were reflected in the water.

"Look, Daddy, it's a full moon."

Jodan and her father grew quiet . . . watching . . . listening. They could almost hear each other's breathing. The cold air blew against their faces.

It was a most happy silence.

Jodan pulled at her father's sleeve.

"Dad?"

"What, Jode?"

"I like you."

He squeezed her hand. "I like you, too."

Sunday. Monday. Tuesday. Wednesday. The time slid by.

Jodan didn't want to leave, but she knew she had to. Besides, she missed her mother.

The last evening of her visit, they went to a restaurant for dinner and Jodan was allowed to choose any dessert she wanted. She had a piece of chocolate cake with strawberry ice cream on it.

Then they came home and packed her suitcase. It was a hard thing to do.

"Hey, Jodan, get ready for bed and come downstairs," said her father. "It's time for the surprise I made for you."

When she came down, he handed her a book. Jodan gasped as she saw the first page.

"Daddy, it says my name. What kind of book is this?"

"Remember how when you were born I invented your name by putting together the names of people who meant a lot to your mother and me? Well, I invented this book something like that. I put together some thoughts and memories and feelings that mean a lot to me and that I wanted you to be able to think about, too. And just as I made your name specially for you, Jode, I made this book specially for you."

They read it together.

A book for Jodan

You've seen the picture I took while
you were getting born. Wow! Was I
glad to see you all there!

Remember the day we went sailing,
and I called you a question
machine?

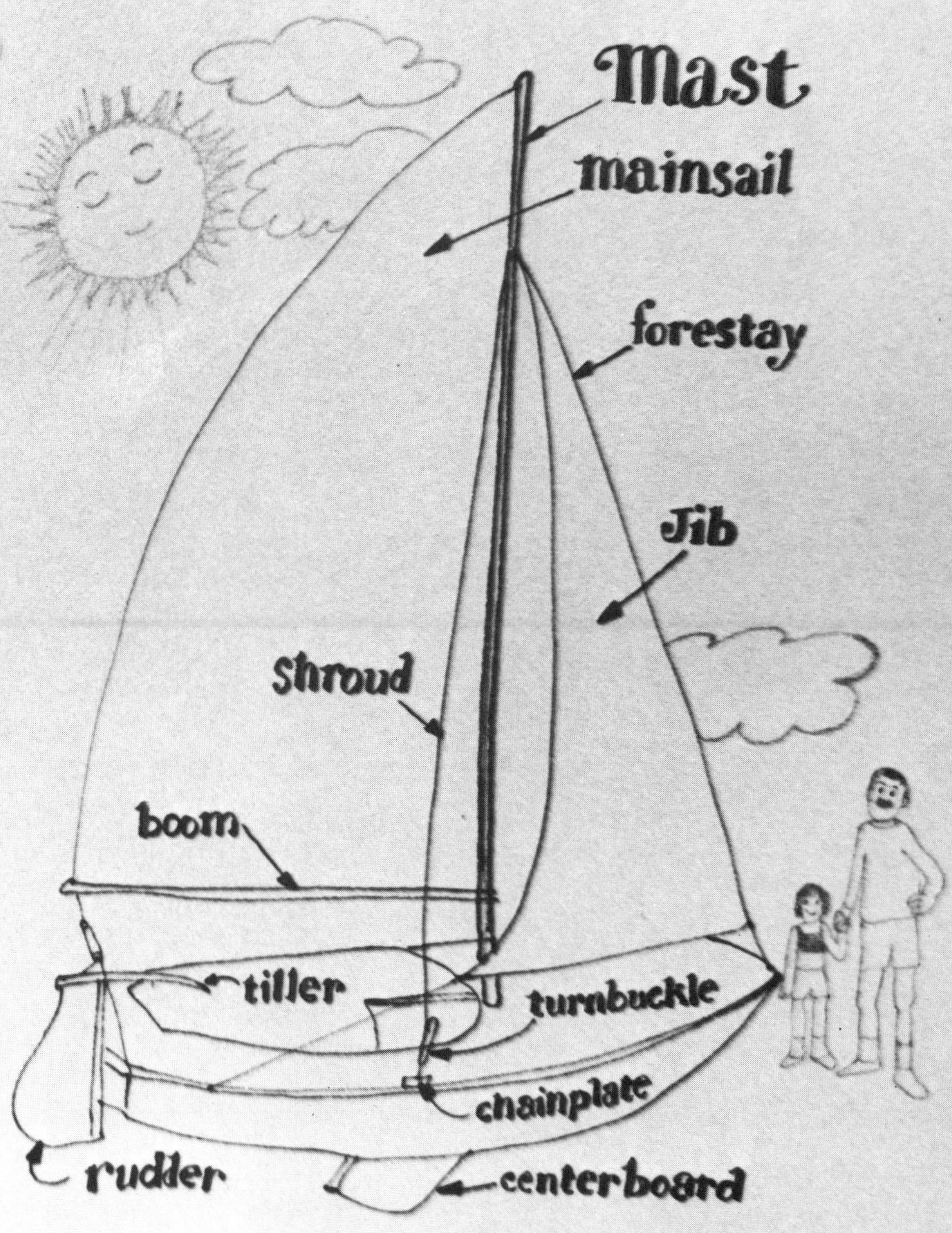

Mast

mainsail

forestay

Jib

shroud

boom

tiller

turnbuckle

chainplate

rudder

centerboard

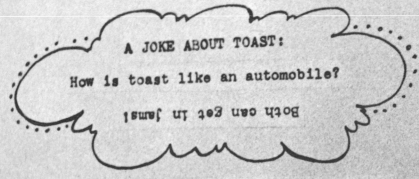

A JOKE ABOUT TOAST:

How is toast like an automobile?

Both can get in jams!

Did you know that I keep these poems you
made up on my bulletin board at work?

1. Twinkle, twinkle little star
What you think is what you are.

(You said that when you were five.)

2. Water buffalo
Better watch out for tigers!
you too elephant!

(That was last year when you were studying
haikus at school.)

Everyone in my office admires them.

This is a picture of a snowflake as seen under a microscope.

Learn to treasure

what is gentle.

Like the snowflake, many gentle things
last only a short time. But do not make
the mistake of thinking that gentle things
are weak or simple.

ADVICE

If something is bothering you, Jodan,
let it out. Don't keep it all smothered
up inside you.

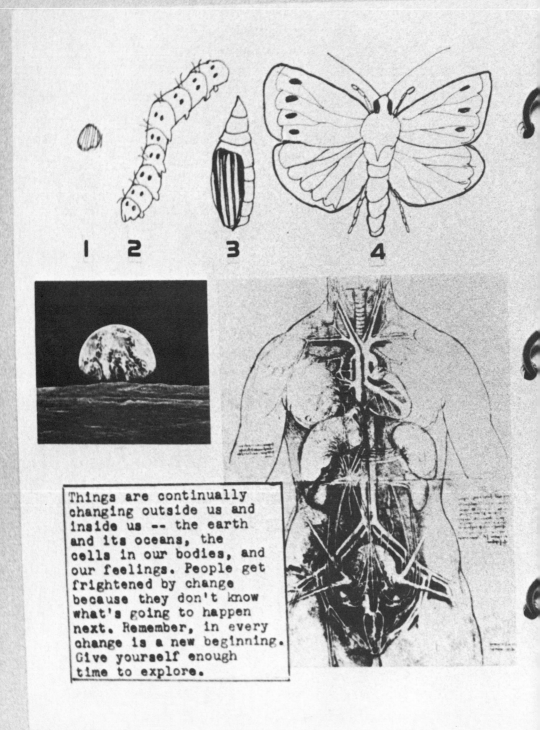

1   2   3   4

Things are continually
changing outside us and
inside us -- the earth
and its oceans, the
cells in our bodies, and
our feelings. People get
frightened by change
because they don't know
what's going to happen
next. Remember, in every
change is a new beginning.
Give yourself enough
time to explore.

There are four animals hidden in this
picture. Can you find them?

(Hint: One of them is an elephant.)

RECIPE

for the pancakes we make together:

1. Beat one **EGG** until fluffy.

2. Add 1 cup of **MILK** to egg.

3. Sift ¾ to 1 cup of **FLOUR**. Add a pinch of **Salt** and 1 tablespoon of **MOLASSES**. Mix all together.

4. Add the flour mixture slowly to the egg batter with 1 tablespoon of melted **butter**.

5. Add X.

6. Cover the batter and let stand for about ¾ of an hour.

7. When ready to fry, blend in ½ teaspoon of baking powder.

(X stands for the secret ingredient.)

RECIPE
for loving something that grows:

When you love something that is alive (like a plant or an animal), try to help it grow and be itself.

First you have to find out what it needs to be healthy. Then you have to give it time to find its own way.

You have to learn ways of knowing how it's doing by looking and touching and smelling and feeling.

It takes quite a bit of time to love something properly. You'll need to be patient.

Loving people is a lot like this. But it's more complicated, and I don't think I could write a recipe for it.

You know that lullaby that you like me to
sing to you. Well, here are the words and
music.

This doesn't mean I'll never sing it to you
again in person, because I will. People
never get too old for lullabies.

A letter:

Dear Jodan,

If something captures your interest,
it's fun to find out more about it --
where it came from, how it works,
how to do it well.

me as a kid

These are some of
the things that
captured me when
I was a kid:

THE PARK
MUSIC
CLIMBING TREES
RUNNING

I hope that there'll be
a lot of things in
your life, Jodan, that
you'll want to find

out more about. Being curious is like giving
yourself a present whenever you want one.

Dad

 A PINK TIDDLYWINK CAME TO BREAKFAST

Jode, I thought this was a good
beginning for a story. What
do you think?

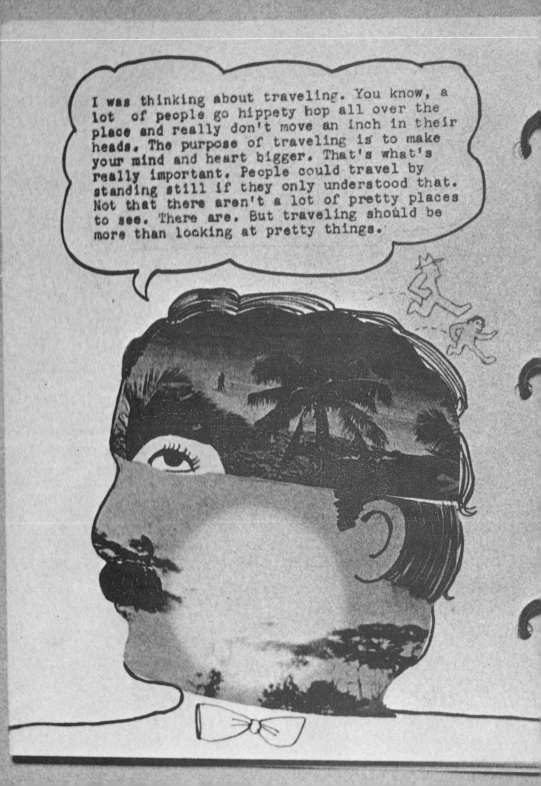

Don't ever forget that we all had good times together. Because it was true. It will help you feel close to other people.

Jodan's father closed the book and put it in Jodan's lap. "Here it is, Jode. It's for you to take with you." Jodan looked up, half laughing, half crying.

"It makes me happy and sad all at the same time. I don't want it to end."

"It's only an end for now, Jode. We can add new parts to it whenever we want to."

"I want to make a book for you."

"I'd like that," said her father. He paused. "Remember that letter you sent telling me how lonely you were for me?" Jodan nodded. She remembered, but she felt far away from those feelings now.

"Well, I wanted you to have something to help you when we're separated again and you miss me."

Jodan snuggled closer to her father.

"I'm really important to you, Daddy, aren't I, even though we're far apart?"

"Very important, Jodan, very important," said her father, and he held her in his arms until she was fast asleep.